Tellwell Talent
www.tellwell.ca

ISBN
978-0-2288-7885-8 (Paperback)
978-0-2288-7886-5 (eBook)

This book is dedicated to my husband,
Tyler and our dog, Frank. I love you both!

Meet Frank; Frank is one of the happiest dogs in the world. He is an only pup who lives with his loving, devoted parents, Mom and Dad.

Frank seemed to be one lucky pup! His parents were amazing! Doting on his every need, making sure each day of his life was his very best...

He was showered with love by his whole family, including all of his cousins.

And knew he only needed to do his "look" to get a second bedtime cookie or a few more cuddles.

Frank was even an active member of the community watch, where he took his job very seriously.

Life was good! So good that Frank wished on a falling star that his life would never change.

The following week Frank found out that he was moving away from his home to a new place. Frank was terrified and started to panic!!!

He overheard his mom say that this new place was out in the middle of nowhere, away from all the "hustle and bustle". She sounded very excited about the move.

But Frank immediately knew what that meant. Now Starbucks would be a 45-minute drive away!

"No more puppacinos whenever I feel like it!!!" Frank gasped when he heard the devastating news. "No more neighborhood watch!!!"

Frank started to think up a plan on how to sabotage the move: but nothing seemed to work.

Then the move happened,
just a few weeks later.

The first few days Frank
protested the move.

But day by day, Frank warmed up to his new home and settled into a new routine.

After a few weeks, Frank came to a new conclusion...

He loved his new home and was happy his parents made this big decision for him!

And he had to agree with his mom, the location was pretty awesome. Family lived in every direction and his presence was requested at every family get together.

Another bonus to the location was the neighbours. There were ducks, geese, moose, and deer always roaming around and eager to play with Frank.

Not to mention Grandma and Grandpa
Garry; their house was close enough that
he could walk there all by himself!

Living next to Grandma and Grandpa had its perks. Every day was filled with new adventures, like making bonfires with Grandpa.

Or feeding the birds with Grandma.

Frank was happy to learn that some old family traditions continued at the new place. Dad still BBQ'd Frank's meals on a regular basis, and Mom still took him for his usual afternoon stroll.

Even puppachinos appeared once in a while!!

One day, while Frank was soaking up some rays in the yard, he started to reminisce about the big move from the city to the country and remembered how scared he had been with all the changes.

... And now, he wouldn't have it any other way.

Manufactured by Amazon.ca
Bolton, ON

28293295R00026